D0963629

ADAPTED BY
TRACEY WEST

SCHOLASTIC INC.
New York   Toronto   London   Auckland   Sydney
Mexico City   New Delhi   Hong Kong

No part of this publication may be reproduced, stored in a retrieval system, or transmitted in any form or by any means, electronic, mechanical, photocopying, recording, or otherwise, without written permission of the publisher. For information regarding permission, write to Scholastic Inc., Attention: Permissions Department, 555 Broadway, New York, NY 10012.

ISBN 0-439-29488-6

12 11 10 9 8 7 6 5 4 3 2 1   1 2 3 4 5 6/0

Printed in the U.S.A.
First Scholastic printing, April 2001

Meet the New Pokémon!

Hello! I am Dexter. I am a kind of computer called a Pokédex. I know facts about all kinds of Pokémon, creatures with special powers.

In this book you will meet some brand-new Pokémon:

Cleffa: This little pink Pokémon is very friendly. Cleffa evolves into Clefairy.

Hitmontop: This Fighting Pokémon spins around on its head like a top.

Hoppip: Each Hoppip's head has two leaves on top. When a wind blows, the Hoppip float away and ride the wind.

Houndour: Do not mess with this Pokémon! Houndour is a Dark-type Pokémon. It looks tough. When it growls, it is not happy.

Igglybuff: What is pale pink, round, and cute? Igglybuff! It evolves into Jigglypuff.

Magby: Magby is packed with fire-power. It evolves into Magmar.

Murkrow: These Dark and Flying Pokémon flock together. They do not like to be disturbed.

Pichu: These Pokémon are known for their playfulness. These adorable Electric Pokémon evolve into Pikachu.

Smoochum: Smoochum looks sweet. It evolves into the strange Pokémon named Jynx. It likes to blow kisses.

You will find more new Pokémon in this book. See if you can count them all!

Chapter One
THE BIG CITY

"Ok, this is it!" said Ash Ketchum.

Pikachu jumped up and down. The little yellow Pokémon was excited. Ash was Pikachu's Pokémon trainer. Ash's friends, Brock, and Misty were with him. They had brought their Pokémon to the big city for a day of fun.

Now they all stood on the roof of a skyscraper. Pikachu looked down at the city. Then Pikachu looked at its friends.

Ash's Pokémon Bulbasaur was blue-green and had a plant bulb on its back. Ash had caught some new Pokémon, too. Chikorita was a light green Grass Pokémon with a leaf on its head. Cyndaquil, a Fire Pokémon, had red spots on its back. Totodile was a light blue

Water Pokémon with rows of sharp teeth. Noctowl had brown feathers and wings. It stared out at the city with big, round eyes.

Misty liked Water Pokémon best. Goldeen had frilly orange fins. Psyduck looked confused. Poliwhirl was a round purple Pokémon with a swirl on its belly. Staryu looked like a star.

Brock had a few Rock Pokémon. Geodude looked like a round rock with two strong arms. Onix looked like a big snake made of rocks. Pineco, a new Bug Pokémon, looked more like a pinecone. It had spiky points all over it. Brock's Zubat flapped its blue wings.

"Now remember, just hang out here while we're gone," Ash told the Pokémon. Then he pointed to a big clock. It could be seen from all over the city.

"See that clock tower over there," Ash said, "we will be back at six o'clock. Until then, you can do anything you want except get in trouble. Have fun!"

Pikachu could not wait to get started.

"Pikachu!" said Pikachu. It was time to have fun!

Chapter Two
TWO PICHU

The Pokémon all headed for a
beautiful park on top of a skyscraper. There was something
there for everyone. The Water
Pokémon swam in a fountain.
Noctowl and Zubat flew through
the trees. Other Pokémon played
on the swings and the slide.

Pikachu climbed up a tall tree. It wanted to try to spot some new Pokémon.

Pikachu did not have to wait long.

"*Piiiiii!*" said a little voice.

Pikachu looked up. Two little yellow Pokémon were standing on a high ledge. They looked like Pikachu, but they were smaller. Their ears were bigger. And their black tails did not look like lightning bolts, like Pikachu's did. These Pokémon looked like brothers.

Pikachu could not believe its eyes. They were Pichu! Pikachu had never met a Pichu before. It knew the Pichu would become Pikachu one day. Pikachu had to talk to them.

"Piiiiii!" One of the Pichu made a face at Pikachu. It stuck out its tongue.

"Piiiiii!" scolded the other Pichu. This one had a tuft of yellow fur on its head. It did not want its brother to tease Pikachu.

Pikachu did not mind. The little Pichu was so silly!

Then the first Pichu stepped off the ledge. It walked onto a metal beam. The beam led from the ledge to another building.

"*Pi pi pi!*" said the brother with the tuft of fur on its head. *That is too dangerous!* it seemed to say.

The Pichu followed its brother onto the beam. The little Pichu teetered. They could not keep their balance.

Pikachu had to do something.

The Pichu were very high. They might fall!

"Pika!" Pikachu climbed down the tall tree and ran to help the Pichu.

Chapter Three
UNHAPPY MURKROW

A flagpole stuck out from the side of the building where Pikachu and the Pokémon were playing. Pikachu climbed out onto the pole.

Pikachu reached out. It could almost touch the Pichu.

"Murkrow! Murkrow!"

Pikachu looked up. A flock of

Dark and Flying Pokémon swooped down from the sky. The Murkrow had blue feathers. They had long, curved beaks.

"Krow! Krow!" screeched the Murkrow. Pikachu had climbed onto their roost. They wanted Pikachu out!

Pikachu held onto the flagpole. The Murkrow pulled on Pikachu's ears and tail.

Pikachu could not hold on any longer. It slipped from the pole.

"Pichu!" The two Pichu screamed as Pikachu fell.

Pikachu thought fast. It grabbed hold of the rope on the flagpole.

Pikachu looked down. The sidewalk looked so far away. Pikachu had to get to safety, fast.

"Murkrow!" One of the Murkrow was still mad. It flew down to the rope. It pecked at the knot that attached the rope to the flagpole.

Pikachu closed its eyes. It knew it was going to fall.

"Pika!" cried Pikachu. So far, it was not having fun in the big city at all!

Chapter Four
HERE COMES HOPPIP

Nearby, Meowth washed the windows of a tall building. The Pokémon had a long tail and two pointed ears. Meowth was part of Team Rocket. Jessie, James, and Meowth tried to steal Pokémon. They really wanted to get their hands on Pikachu.

However, Team Rocket was not very good at stealing Pokémon. They took a job washing windows to make extra money.

"When Jessie and James said they found me a job where I'd start at the top and clean up," said Meowth. "I didn't know they had this in mind!"

Meowth looked down. The wooden platform hung from ropes. It was very high above the ground.

Pikachu had its own worries. It tried to hang onto the flagpole rope. But the Murkrow pecked and pecked.

Suddenly, Pikachu saw a strange sight. Many round pink Pokémon were floating toward it. They were riding on the wind.

"Hoppip," sang the Pokémon as they flew.

The Hoppip floated right to Pikachu. Up close, they looked like soft, comfy pillows.

Boing! Three Hoppip bounced on the Murkrow that was pecking at the knot in the rope. The

Murkrow finished pecking at the rope and flew away.

Yay! Pikachu was safe. But not for long.

The rope was untied! Pikachu was falling.

Pikachu closed its eyes.

Boink! Pikachu landed on something soft.

Pikachu opened its eyes. It had landed on a Hoppip. Pikachu bounced up and came down. It landed on another Hoppip.

Pikachu bounced from Hoppip to Hoppip.

"Piiiiii!" cheered the Pichu from the ledge. The Hoppip had saved Pikachu from falling!

Pikachu bounced one last time. It landed on Meowth's platform.

"Pikachu?" Meowth could not believe its eyes. The platform bounced up like a seesaw. Meowth went flying through the air.

"I'm blasting off again!" Meowth cried.

Pikachu climbed off the plat-form and up to the roof. It ran to the Pichu.

Pikachu had to think of a safe

way down. Maybe its friends could help them. Bulbasaur, Onix, and the others would know what to do. Pikachu spotted the other Poké-mon across the street in the park on top of the other building.

"Pikaaaaaaaa!" Pikachu called. But they could not hear it.

"Pichu! Pichu!" The little Pichu tugged at Pikachu's arm. They seemed to be saying, *We know a way down.* They ran across the ledge.

"Pika!" Pikachu ran after the two little Pichu.

Chapter Five
ALL WET

The Pichu opened up a metal vent in the side of the building. They jumped inside.

Pikachu jumped in behind them. It was dark and spooky inside the vent.

The brothers were not scared.

They slid down the vent. Pikachu slid after them.

Pikachu could see bright sunlight ahead. The vent opened up. They were going to slide outside!

Pikachu could not stop. The Pichu flew out of the vent. Pikachu followed. It felt like it was falling again.

A city bus rode past them. Pikachu and the Pichu landed right on top.

"Pichu!" said the Pichu. They smiled.

Then the bus made a sharp turn. Pikachu and the Pichu were not holding on. They flew off the bus!

Splash! They landed in a lake. Pikachu opened its eyes. Strange blue Pokémon swam in the water. They were round. Tiny flippers pushed them through the water.

"Chinchou," said the Pokémon. Bubbles came from their mouths as they spoke.

Pikachu could not stay under-water much longer. Pikachu and the Pichu swam to the top of the lake. They were safe!

But not for long. A big blue boat sailed across the lake. It was shaped like a Lapras. The boat was headed right for them.

"Pikachu!" cried Pikachu.

Pikachu and the brothers grabbed a piece of wood. Pikachu paddled with all its might. The Lapras boat was right behind them.

Suddenly, a giant Pokémon called a Gyarados rose out of the water. Gyarados looked like a sea monster. Gyarados made a wave that carried Pikachu and the Pichu up, up, and out of the lake.

The three Electric Pokémon landed on top of Houndour. Pikachu looked at the brothers. Thank goodness! They were all right.

"Houndour!"

The Dark Pokémon was not happy. It looked tough! It had jet-black hair and a red belly. Houndour growled. Pikachu could see its white teeth.

"Houndour!" Houndour sounded angry. It growled again.

Then it began chasing Pikachu and the Pichu!

Chapter Six
ESCAPE FROM HOUNDOUR

Pikachu and Pichu turned and raced down an alley.

Pikachu spotted a clothesline. Maybe Houndour could not climb after them.

Pikachu and the Pichu climbed

up the clothesline. Then they ran on top of the ropes.

But Houndour was fast. It followed the Electric Pokémon. It raced along the ground beneath the ropes.

Towels fell off the clothesline as the brothers ran. The towels covered Houndour's face.

Pikachu and the Pichu reached the end of the clothesline. They jumped down the other end.

Pikachu and the Pichu kept running. They ran to the end of the alley. A fence blocked their way.

Will Pikachu make new friends on its trip to the city?

Yippee! The Pokémon are going to the big city. Goldeen, Pineco, Zubat, Poliwhirl, Onix, Psyduck, and Staryu are ready for their adventure.

Pikachu is on top of the world!

Cyndaquil, Totodile, Geodude, Noctowl, Vulpix, Bulbasaur, Chikorita, Pikachu, and Togepi get ready to play.

These two Pichu like to play. But they can get into lots of trouble.

Three Murkrow peck at Pikachu.

Pikachu hops from Hoppip to Hoppip.

Pikachu is safe, but . . .

Meowth is blasting off again!

Run, Pikachu, run!
Pikachu plays with
its new friends.

Pikachu and the Pichu slide down a vent.
What a fun game!

Run, run, as fast as you can!
Houndour is coming!

Time for teamwork.
A Thundershock
from the Pichu stops
Houndour in its tracks.

Pikachu and the Pichu find a tower made of tires. Smeargle greets them.

The Wooper want to play.

Spinarak and a group of Sunflora are happy to meet Pikachu.

Hoppip float on air.

Hitmontop shows off its Rapid Spin Move. Shuckle watches.

Oh no! The tower tumbles.

Pikachu to the rescue!
Pikachu protects the Pichu
and helps save the tower.

The tower is safe! Cleffa, Igglybuff, Magby, and Furrett are happy.

What a fun place to play! Pikachu wishes it could stay all day . . .

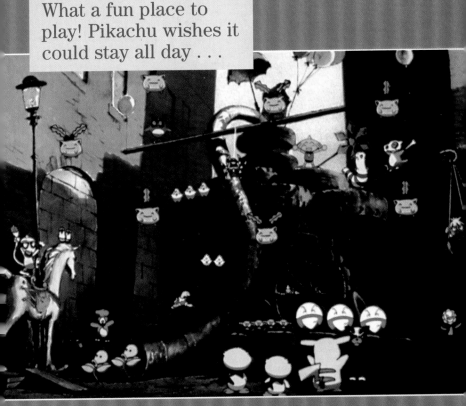

But Pikachu must get back
to Ash. The Pichu know a
quick way.

Time for Pikachu and the Pichu to say good-bye.

Surprise! It's a Pokémon friendship party!
The gang is all here.

Ash is having a
party for Pikachu
to celebrate
the day they met.
Pikachu is a good
friend.

"Houndour!" The Houndour had found them.

Pikachu and the Pichu were trapped. The fence was behind them. The Houndour was in front of them. There was nowhere to go.

The two Pichu held hands. They squeezed their eyes tight.

"Pichuuuuuuuuuu!"

The little Pichu were hitting Houndour with a double Electric Attack!

The Pichu attack started as a small sizzle. Then it grew to a ball of yellow energy.

The electric blast hit Houndour. It frazzled the Pokémon.

The brothers fell to the ground and fainted. The attack had weakened them.

Pikachu picked up both of them. This was their chance to get away!

Pikachu climbed up the fence.

"Houndour!" Behind them, Houndour growled. It had recovered from the attack.

Pikachu knew it had to jump. It looked down.

Pikachu smiled. A big, chubby Snorlax slept below. Pikachu knew

about Snorlax. The sleeping Pokémon had a very bouncy belly.

"*Pika!*"

Pikachu held the brothers
tightly and jumped.

Boing! They bounced off Snorlax's belly and ran away.

Behind them, Houndour
climbed the fence. Houndour got
ready to jump, too.

Snorlax snored. Then it rolled
over.

Crash! Houndour landed on the
hard concrete instead of on Snorlax's soft belly.

Squish! Snorlax rolled over —
right on top of Houndour!
Houndour was not going anywhere
for a while.

Pikachu leaned against a building. It put down the little Pichu.

The Pokémon were awake now.
They jumped up and down. The
brothers were excited.

"Pichu. Chu, chu," said the
Pichu. They took Pikachu by the
hand. They led Pikachu around a
corner.

Pikachu gasped. The Pichu had
led them to a lot. Inside the lot

was the most amazing thing Pikachu had ever seen. Someone had built a huge playhouse out of old tires and pipes. A tall tower rose from the bottom of the play-house. Pikachu knew it must be a special place.

"*Pichu, pichu!*" said the Pichu.

Chapter Seven

POKéMON
PLAYHOUSE

"Pichu!" called the brothers.
Suddenly, the playground came
to life. Pokémon popped out of
every corner. Pikachu had never

seen some of them before. The Pichu told Pikachu their names as each one said hello.

First Cubone swung by on a rope. Then Smeargle ran by and waved. The little Pokémon was white with brown markings.

Then Magby popped out of an old tire and waved. Magby had dark pink feathers, a yellow belly, and a sweet face.

Igglybuff twirled around on its tiny feet. The puffy pale pink Pokémon had big pink eyes.

Smoochum called from the top of the tower. With its yellow hair and pink face, it looked sweet. Smoochum blew a big kiss to Pikachu.

Furret scampered in and out of the tires. The furry Pokémon had a long, sleek body. Red-brown stripes marked its white fur.

A chubby pink Cleffa hopped from foot to foot. Triangle-shaped ears stuck out on either side of its head.

Then Pikachu saw some Pokémon that it recognized. A Voltorb

rolled down the pipes. It looked like a red-and-white Poké Ball. Two Rattata jumped out of a stack of tires. A Bellsprout walked along on its stem-like body. And three little blue Oddish danced around the playhouse. The green leaves on their heads swayed back and forth.

But that was not the end of the new Pokémon. Three Sunflora popped out of some empty wood barrels. The cheerful Pokémon had gold petals that circled their smiling faces.

Another new Pokémon popped out of the last barrel — Spinarak, a green Bug Pokémon with eight legs.

Then the Pichu pointed to some old pipes. One by one, six Wooper jumped up out of the pipes. *"Woop! Woop! Woop!"* they cheered. Each Wooper had a round face, a short body, and a flat tail. Spiky sticks stuck out from each side of its head. The funny-looking Pokémon made Pikachu giggle.

All of the Pokémon began to run around and play. More Hoppip floated in the air. A Pokémon with a long neck and a round red body played hide-and-seek with a Bellsprout. *"Shuckle! Shuckle!"* said the Pokémon.

A Pokémon with a point on top of its head ran up to Pikachu and the Pichu. Hitmontop flipped upside down. It began to spin on its head like a top.

The brothers let out a happy cry. They grabbed Pikachu and jumped onto Hitmontop's feet. Hitmontop twirled around. It was like riding a merry-go-round.

Hitmontop spun faster and faster. Pikachu and the Pichu flew off. They landed on top of a long pipe.

"Pichu!" screamed the Pichu happily. They all slid down the pipe. The pipe twisted and curved like a roller coaster.

Pikachu and the Pichu landed on one-half of a seesaw. A little Wooper sat on the other end. When the three Electric Pokémon landed, the Wooper flew straight up. Then ten more Wooper came back down! Now it was Pikachu and the Pichu's turn to fly off the seesaw.

The three yellow Pokémon flew up to the tower. They landed inside a big, old clock. The clock gears turned and whirred. The little Pichu rolled from one gear to the next. Smoochum, Bellsprout, Spinarak, and Magby were all riding on the gears, too.

Then a loud bell rang in the city. The Pokémon stopped playing. They began to climb out of the playhouse.

"Pichu pichu," said the brothers.

Pikachu waved good-bye to its new friends. Then it remembered something.

Pikachu looked at the big clock in the middle of the city. The two hands were almost at six o'clock.

Pikachu had to get back to Ash!

Chapter Eight
LOOK OUT, HOUNDOUR!

Pikachu and the Pichu started
to run away from the playhouse.

"Houndour!"

Oh, no! Houndour was back.
And it looked angrier than ever.

Pikachu and the Pichu ran
away. They ran over garbage cans.

They ran over pipes. They ran all around the playhouse. Houndour ran right behind them.

Pikachu ran up the tower made of tires. Then it jumped back down to the ground.

Houndour jumped, too. Its strong paws kicked the tires as it took a big leap.

Suddenly, Pikachu heard a rumbling sound. The playhouse began to shake. It was going to fall.

Pika! thought Pikachu.

Pikachu grabbed the Pichu. It tried to jump out of the way.

Too late! The pipes broke into pieces. The stacks of old tires came apart. The tires and pipes tumbled down to the ground. They buried Pikachu and the Pichu.

"Pikachu!" Pikachu pulled itself and the brothers out of the pile of tires. They were not hurt. But where was Houndour?

"Hound!" Houndour popped its head out of a tire. It smiled at Pikachu and the Pichu. *"Houndour! Houndour!"* It seemed to be saying, *I am sorry. I did not mean to hurt anybody!*

Pikachu smiled back. It was glad Houndour wanted to be friends.

But their problems were not over. The bottom of the playhouse had fallen apart. Now the tall tower rocked in the wind.

The tower was going to topple over!

Chapter Nine
TEAMWORK

Houndour ran to the tower. It pushed against the tires. It wanted to hold up the tower so it would not fall.

Pikachu saw that a rope connected the tower to a pipe on the ground. The rope was slipping. Pikachu ran and grabbed the rope.

Houndour was strong. Pikachu was smart to grab the rope. But the two of them could not save the tower by themselves.

The brothers called for help. *"Pichu! Chu chu!"*

In a flash, the Pokémon came back to the playhouse. They all ran to help. The two Pichu grabbed the rope with Pikachu. Hitmontop, Igglybuff, Furret, Cubone, Cleffa, and Oddish grabbed the rope, too.

Bellsprout threw a long green vine at the tower. Spinarak spun a white, sticky thread at the tower and threw it like a rope. The vine and the thread helped keep the tower steady.

Other Pokémon helped, too. They piled the tires back onto the playhouse. Sunflora, Smoochum, and Cleffa threw the tires back on, one by one.

Pikachu felt the rope start to slip. They only had to hold on a little longer. Soon there would be enough tires piled up to hold up the tower. They just needed a little more time. . . .

Snap! The rope broke in half. Pikachu and the other Pokémon holding the rope went flying.

The Pokémon landed safely on the ground. But the tower groaned. It was going to fall!

Houndour pushed with all its might to hold up the tower. The Pokémon on the ground worked harder to pile up tires. Hitmontop spun on its top. It tossed tires onto the pile with its feet. Magby blasted the metal pipes with its fire breath. It welded the broken pipes back together.

Other Pokémon formed an assembly line. Igglybuff passed a tire to Bellsprout. Bellsprout passed a tire to Smoochum. They piled up the tires faster than before.

Finally, all the tires were back in place. The pipes were back together. The tower stopped teetering.

The Pokémon had saved the playhouse!

"Pichu!"

"Hitmontop!"

"Smoochum!"

"Woop! Woop!"

All of the Pokémon let out a cheer.

Pikachu cheered the loudest. Saving the playground felt great!

Chapter Ten
TIME TO GO

Pikachu could have stayed at the playhouse all day. But it did not forget about Ash.

Bells rang in the clock tower. Pikachu looked at the clock. The two hands were almost together! It had to hurry.

"Pikachu! Pika pika!" Pikachu

waved good-bye to its friends one last time.

Then Pikachu raced down the alley. The skyscraper was so far away. It would never make it!

Then Pikachu saw something out of the corner of its eye. The two Pichu had jumped into an old tire. The tire sped down the street.

"Pichu! Pi!" they called.

Pikachu hopped in the tire. The street turned into a steep hill. The tire raced down the hill at super-speed.

Meowth was walking up the hill. The pooped Pokémon was trying to get back to Jessie and James.

"After a horrible day," said Meowth. "I sure could use a little boost."

Pikachu could not control the tire. The tire slammed right into Meowth! Poor Meowth flew high in the air. It landed right back on the platform where it had been washing windows.

"I need a doctor!" said Meowth.

Back in the street, the tire rolled and rolled. Then it bounced to a stop — right in front of the skyscraper!

Pikachu jumped out. The Pichu and Pikachu ran inside and hopped on the elevator.

The elevator stopped at the roof of the skyscraper. Pikachu ran out. All of the other Pokémon were back. The two Pichu waved good-bye.

Pikachu smiled. It would miss these cute Pichu. They were so friendly. And they had shown Pikachu that the big city could be a very fun place.

But Ash was very important to Pikachu.

"Pikachu! Pika pi!" called Pikachu. It seemed to be saying, *I will miss you! I will try to come back someday!*

Chapter Eleven
PIKA PARTY!

Ash, Brock, and Misty were on top of the skyscraper, too. Ash smiled when he saw Pikachu.

Ash led everyone through a doorway. The doors led inside a big room. Pikachu gasped. The room was filled with balloons and decorations. There were tables loaded with food. Pikachu saw cakes, fruit, and other yummy things.

"Ash planned this for weeks!" said Misty.

"An extra-special day deserves an extra-special party," added Brock.

"*Pika pi?*" Pikachu asked Ash.

"Do you know what day today is, Pikachu?" Ash asked.

Pikachu shook its head.

"Today is the day we first met. It is the day we first became friends," said Ash. "I think that is very special!"

Pikachu jumped into Ash's arms. Ash remembered!

Ash put his red-and-white cap on Pikachu's head.

"Thanks for being my friend Pikachu," Ash said.

"Pikachu!" agreed Pikachu. The big city was fun. But being Ash's Pokémon was the most fun of all!